Choose Your Days

Choose Your Days

Written and illustrated by

Paula S. Wallace

Be kind.

Sing.

Travel across the street and around the world.

Look at stars.

Listen to birds.

Laugh with your friends.

Learn something new.

Tell people you love them.

DEDICATED WITH GRATITUDE to all loved ones
—near or far, present or absent—
who have lived their days with courage,
compassion, and curiosity.

When she was born, Corky was given
calendars for all of her days by Old Bear,
keeper of time and keys.

She was also given a list—to dream
and to do—to mark each day and
to name each line.

From the wall of names, Old Bear took her key.
"Choose your days, make them sunny or gray,"
he whispered.

60's

70's

80's

"Choose your days,"
she whispered back.

Get up! Get up! You have stuff to do.

She grew.

And she grew.

And she grew.

And the days flew
until only a few remained.

Now she was a little bent and a little gray

and wanted still to fill her day.

With her small purse of coins,
she asked Old Bear for a bit more time.

For work undone. For play postponed.
For music unsung.

Old Bear leaned in close to hear her plea.
"You hold the key," he reminded her.

"Choose your days,
make them sunny or gray."

"And when the play is played."

"And the songs are sung."

"When the seas are sailed."

"And the work is done."

"Go to the dark cottage. Unlock the door—
the door to wonder."

DO NOT
BE AFRAID

"Do not be afraid.
I will wait for you there."

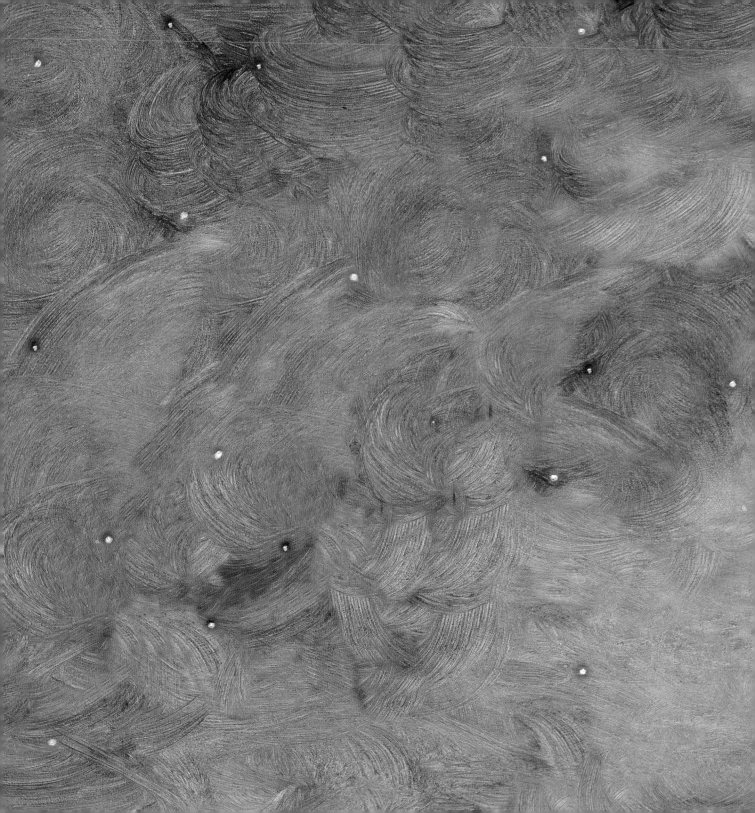